Cherokee Animal Tales

Edited with an Introduction by
GEORGE F. SCHEER

Cherokee
Animal
Tales

Illustrated by
ROBERT FRANKENBERG

HOLIDAY HOUSE, INC. • NEW YORK

Contents

About the Cherokee

Instead of beginning, "Once upon a time," the Cherokee storytellers began their tales by saying, "This is what the old men told me when I was a boy." The old men were the keepers of tribal traditions, but they were not historians. And the Cherokee never painted their history on sticks or wove it into wampum. So no account of their origins has been preserved. No one knows certainly when the first of them came to make their home in the lofty heights of the southern Appalachians. Modern scholars associate them with the mighty Iroquois and suppose they migrated southward from the Great Lakes region in the thirteenth century. There is reason to believe that they swiftly established their dominion over forty thousand square miles of that great forest-clad mountain range which extends southward from western

Virginia through the back country of the Carolinas and eastern Tennessee into northern Georgia and the northeast tip of Alabama.

Sometime, their tribal name was Tsalagi, whose common translation is "cave people," or mountaineers; and aptly enough, for they were truly a mountain people, hardy, self-reliant, both gentle and fierce. Their first devotion was to warfare, which they called their "beloved occupation," and they did everything to aggrandize it by dances, honorary titles, and tribal prestige. But when they were not at war with neighboring tribes or invaders, their men were on the hunt for the game of the highlands. As time passed, they became increasingly agricultural and, in the sunny coves and by the mountain streams, they constructed permanent villages of mud-covered, bark-roofed log huts. Each settlement was commanded by a huge, flat-topped, earthen mound on which stood the townhouse, or council house, where the elders met to make community decisions. But they left to their women the seed-planting, cultivating, and care of stock. And to their women they left the other tasks of homesteading, the cooking and housekeeping, the rearing of children, the smoking of meats, the tanning of hides, and the making of clothes.

The first white men to come among the Cherokee were the Spanish; and with their coming the Cherokee entered written history.

On May 30, 1540, the conquistador, Hernando De Soto,

10

leading an expedition of armored soldiers, tarnished and tattered from months in the American wilderness, tramped into a Cherokee village in the North Carolina highlands. For nearly a year, De Soto, hungrily searching for riches, had stabbed northward and westward from his landing at Tampa Bay. Although in his retinue were several hundred shackled, burdened Indians he had captured or bought from their chiefs, his stay at the Cherokee town of Guasili was entirely friendly. After a brief rest, he quietly turned his men down the western slopes toward Tennessee. Sixteen years later, another conquistador, Juan Prado, penetrated the Cherokee country. The Cherokee appeared in the Spaniards' vague and contradictory narratives of their explorations; and then a century passed before white men saw them again.

On a pleasant July day in 1673, there appeared in a Cherokee village on the Little Tennessee River two men, come as traders to open a path between the "Overhills" Cherokee capital of Chota and the colony of Virginia. By now Jamestown was flourishing and the Virginians were moving up the rivers toward the interior, and colonists were building their first dwellings on South Carolina's Ashley River. As more and more traders visited the Cherokee, sometimes coming to live among them, Indian and white associations became fairly common. But the Cherokee remained by choice savage. And as white hunters climbed into the game-laden mountains, as outreaching settlers squatted in Cherokee forests, and the English and the French of the Ohio Valley

11

competed for the friendship of the Cherokee, the Cherokee found themselves in everlasting dispute over boundaries and loyalties.

They made their first inevitable land cession to the white man in 1721, when they deeded to the English Crown some fifty square miles on the western border of South Carolina. It was a negotiation that served well the purpose of English colonial expansion, but it also was the first of what became a woeful succession of treaties which, in little more than a century, claimed all the homeland of the Cherokee. Nine years later, the Cherokee reaffirmed this first treaty and pledged their eternal allegiance to the King of England, whom seven of their leaders traveled to London to visit. Despite this declaration of fealty, however, they continued to fight every English encroachment, until the American Revolution.

Following the Revolution, the new American government issued proclamations protecting the Cherokee from land-grabbers, but the Confederation was too weak to enforce its own proclamations. With the inauguration of George Washington, the founding of a new, stronger government, and the negotiation in 1791 of what promised to be a sound treaty, the Cherokee began to believe they could live out their lives on their own lands unmolested. However, they also realized that they must learn to accommodate to the white man's world and to the problems posed for them by its dominance and strength; so, at last, accepting the aid of white missionaries and the encouragement of the federal government, they embarked upon peaceful rural pursuits and placed themselves under the protection of the United States Congress. They built roads, schools, and churches, modernized their agriculture, and began patterning their local government on that of the United States.

Much of the remarkable progress they made in the early years of the nineteenth century stemmed from the invention, over a period of twelve years, of a Cherokee syllabary, or syllabic alphabet, by a crippled hunter named Sequoyah. Its eighty-five characters represented all the sounds of the Cherokee language, and it made possible the keeping of lasting tribal records and the publishing in Cherokee of books and eventually of a newspaper. So entranced were the Cherokee with the idea of a written language of their own and so eager for learning that in a few months after the publication of Sequoyah's alphabet in 1821, thousands of former illiterates were able to read and write.

But for all of the government's reassurances and all of the Cherokees' efforts to conform to the demands of the white man's society, one federal administration after another—by methods brutal, deceptive, and disillusioning—forced the Cherokee to cede more and more land. Between 1794 and 1819, the United States government pressed them into making twenty-four separate land cessions; by treaties first with the English and then with the United States, they had ceded, by 1820, nearly half their original forty-thousand-square-mile domain. The truth began to emerge that nothing less than "removal" of the Cherokee from the eastern United States could mitigate the lust of settlers and land speculators. In the next few years about a quarter of the Cherokee Nation, as they called themselves under their new constitution, some six thousand, unwilling to give up the free life of their ancestors—and perhaps anticipating their ultimate fate—voluntarily left their nation and trekked westward beyond the Mississippi. But the majority dug in, determined to hold to their mist-capped mountains.

Despoliation of the Cherokee undoubtedly was accelerated with the election, in 1828, of Andrew Jackson, a remorseless Indian-hater. In his first annual message to Congress, he announced his intention of getting a bill in the first session for removal of all the southeastern Indians to west of the Mississippi. Georgia, which since 1802 had spearheaded a drive to oust the Indians, immediately intensified its campaign for removal. In 1830 Jackson got his Indian Removal Bill which provided for "treaties" of removal. Choctaws, Creeks, Chickasaws, and Seminoles broke under this pressure from the federal government, signed documents, and started westward. The Cherokee resisted and carried their cause to the United States Supreme Court. When the Court upheld their position, Jackson refused to recognize the decision.

The Cherokee made one last plea to the United States Congress. The Congress did nothing. In 1835, by dividing the Cherokee into factions, Jackson forced through a treaty

14

under which the Cherokee agreed to exchange their empire in the East for five million dollars and land beyond the Mississippi. Although many leaders of the Cherokee Nation and the majority of its citizens did not consider the Treaty of New Echota to be binding, the United States government did.

For two years the Cherokee ignored the treaty some of their leaders had signed. Then units of the United States Army were sent into the mountains to round up the Cherokee—men, women, and children—herd them into wagons, and escort them to "the Indian Territory."

Some fourteen thousand began the terrible eight-hundred-mile journey. In the six months it took them to reach the West, almost a fourth died of famine, illness, and fatigue. A young American soldier from Tennessee, Captain John Burnett, who had lived and hunted and fished with the Cherokee, was sent along as an interpreter. Years later he recalled seeing "the helpless Cherokee arrested and dragged from their homes and driven at the bayonet point into stockades. And in the chill of a drizzling rain, on an October morning, I saw them loaded like cattle or sheep into 645 wagons and started toward the west."

Sleet and snow swirled down on the morning of November 17 and, Captain Burnett recalled, "from that day until we reached the end of the fateful journey on March 26th, 1839, the sufferings of the Cherokee were awful. The trail of the exiles was a trail of death. . . . The long painful journey ... ended ... with four thousand silent graves reaching from the foothills of the Smokey Mountains [in North Carolina] to ... the Indian Territory."

The Cherokee called it the Trail of Tears. Its survivors built in the West a new, self-governing nation. They again built roads, schools, and churches and laid down farms and ranches.

The Civil War divided the Cherokee Nation, but when it was over the Cherokee repaired the devastation it had wrought and for forty years kept their republic alive and at peace. Though money was "as scarce as angels' wings," according to the Cherokee newspaper, a home for the indigent, a telephone exchange, and an opera house were but a few of their achievements. Eventually, however, as the twentieth century opened, the old tribal government was dissolved, the property of the Cherokee Nation was divided equitably among its citizens, and in 1907 the western Cherokee territory was absorbed by the new state of Oklahoma.

But the chronicle of the Cherokee does not end in Oklahoma. Not all of them traveled the Trail of Tears. When the Army came into the Appalachians in 1838, about a thousand of them hid in the secret places of the silent Great Smokies of North Carolina. These homeless, penniless fugitives might not have survived but for the friendship of one William H. Thomas, a white trader who, after twenty years among them, had the full confidence of the mountain Cherokee. On their behalf Thomas persisted for four years until he got the permission of the federal government for them to remain in the Smokies. To him, as agent and trustee for the Cherokee, the government paid what it owed them under the treaty of removal. Since the state of North Carolina did not recognize Indians as landowners, Thomas bought land for them in his own name on Oconaluftee River, Soco Creek, and farther west.

These lands, too, were endangered when Thomas, aged and ill, was beset by creditors who considered the lands he held in trust to be part of his encumbered estate. However, at this point, the government intervened on behalf of the Cherokee and appointed the United States Commissioner of Indian Affairs their trustee.

In 1875, the Cherokee adopted a constitution under which the government would do business with them; and the next year they were granted title to their own lands, eighty-six square miles, embracing the area known as the Qualla Boundary and outlying tracts. In 1889, some years after their legal ties to the western Cherokee had been broken, the Eastern Band of Cherokees was empowered by the state of North Carolina to conduct their affairs as a tribe. And in 1925 the tribal council transferred title of its lands to the federal government, which today holds them in trust for the benefit of the band.

With a heritage of industriousness, today's Cherokee are engaged in much the same occupations as their fellow Americans. They farm, manage their forests, make handicraft

17

articles, work in manufacturing plants within the Boundary, and cater to about five million tourists a year, who come to observe their festivals, enjoy their crafts, and roam their spectacular hills, streams, and forests.

II

Although the origin of the Cherokee and the facts of their history before the coming of the white man are lost, fragments of their ancient culture survive. Their beadwork, wood carvings, fabrics, and especially their basketry still engage them. Some of their traditional games still are played. Old dances still are performed and primeval ceremonies still are held. And much of their mythology, folklore, and pagan religious belief has been preserved.

It is to James Mooney that we owe much of what we know about the historical life and the culture of the Cherokee. Mooney, native of Indiana, developed an abiding interest in Indians as a boy. At the age of twenty-four, after a time of teaching, he set out to study at first hand the Indians of Brazil. However, he chose to travel via Washington, D.C., where Major John Wesley Powell persuaded him to join the Bureau of American Ethnology of the Smithsonian Institution, and he remained in its employ the rest of his life.

In the summer of 1887, Mooney, "a true Irish type" of

medium build with happy gray eyes, dark hair, and a winning way, journeyed into the remote back country of North Carolina to study the language, lore, and material culture of the Cherokee. By that time, said Mooney, the Cherokee had become "undoubtedly the most important tribe in the United States, as well as one of the most interesting. . . ." In wealth, intelligence, and general adaptability to civilization, he said, "they are far ahead of any other of our tribes. . . . They . . . number in all about two thousand. . . . Very few know enough English to converse intelligently. Remaining in their native mountains, away from railroads and progressive white civilization, they retain many customs and traditions which have been lost by those who removed to the West. They still keep up their old dances and ball-plays—although these have been sadly degenerated—their medicine-men, conjurings, songs and legends. . . ."

Mooney's interpreter on the Qualla reservation was a bright young Cherokee named Will West Long, who had endured briefly the white man's school at Trinity College in High Point before returning forever to the isolation of Big Cove. With Long at his side, Mooney put into English a wealth of mythology, folk belief, and oral tradition that he gathered from the then aged and respected storytellers of the tribe, bearing such names as John Ax, Swimmer, and the Chosen One. Later he visited the western Cherokee where he heard other stories, and sometimes slightly different versions of these.

Mooney published his findings in 1900 under the title, *The Myths of the Cherokee*, in the 19th Annual Report of the Bureau of American Ethnology. From them are selected the animal tales found in this volume. They are published here almost exactly as they appear in Mooney's magnificent work. An occasional word has been changed to provide clarity to today's young reader, and a few mechanical changes have been made for ease of reading. But essentially these simple but robust little tales appear here just as they were told originally to James Mooney by the Cherokee and set down by his pen.

All these stories, of course, are laid in the long, long ago. Then, the Cherokee believed, the animals were bigger, stronger, and more perfect than their counterparts of today. They mingled on equal terms with human beings and spoke the same language. They were organized into a society which resembled that of the Cherokee themselves. They had chiefs and councils that met in townhouses and conducted clan and tribal affairs. Each had an individual responsibility in his clan and tribe. The frog, for instance, was the leader in council; the rabbit was the messenger and usually led the dances.

To the Cherokee the rabbit—as he was in primitive cultures around the world—was the great trickster who occasionally was outtricked by the others. He figures prominently in Cherokee tales, as he does in tales from West Africa, Korea, and elsewhere. That such tales are seldom unique is a truism. The story of the rabbit and the tar wolf, popular with generations of American children as a tale of Joel Chandler Harris' Uncle Remus, is told here in a much older version—but very probably long before the Cherokee related it around their fires, it was being told around the fires of other peoples in distant nameless lands. The same might be said, of course, for the story of the rabbit and his race with the terrapin, as well as others.

The animals in Cherokee tales perform impossible feats and are endowed with supernatural powers, and this, too, is perfectly in the tradition of the Cherokees' own medicine men and conjurers.

The animals danced often, as indeed did the Cherokee. Whenever a council was called, it was the occasion for a series of dances, accompanied by feasting and a general good time. Dances figure prominently in the stories told here: dances at council meetings, spontaneous dances such as the one the groundhog devised to save his life, and the immensely popular Green Corn Dance that came at end of summer, "Roasting Ear's Time," to celebrate the harvest.

The animals of the Cherokee tales are gone. In some lost time and in some unexplained way, the Cherokee say, they left this lower world and ascended to the world above that the Cherokee call Galunlati, and there they still exist. The animals we know came to earth as imitations of the great ones that had been before. Happily, James Mooney preserved forever the lives and antics of the great ones.

Cherokee
Animal
Tales

The First Fire

In the beginning there was no fire. The world was cold, until the Thunders who lived above sent their lightning and put fire into the bottom of a hollow sycamore tree which grew on an island. The animals knew the fire was there, because they could see the smoke coming out at the top of the tree, and they wanted it to warm themselves. But they could not get to it because of the water. So they held a council to decide what to do. This was a long time ago.

Every animal that could fly or swim was eager to go after the fire. The Raven offered to go and, because he was so large and strong, all the others thought he

could do the work. So he was sent first. He flew high and far across the water and alighted on the sycamore tree. But while he was wondering what to do, the heat scorched all his feathers black, and he was frightened and came back without the fire.

The little Screech Owl volunteered to go and reached the island safely. But while he was looking down into the hollow tree, a blast of hot air came up and nearly burned out his eyes. He flew home as best he could, but it was a long time before he could see well. And his eyes are red to this day.

Then the Hooting Owl and the Horned Owl went. But by the time they got to the hollow tree, the fire was burning so fiercely the smoke nearly blinded them, and the ashes carried up by the wind made white rings around their eyes. They had to come home without the fire. And for all their rubbing, they were never able to get rid of the white rings.

Now no more of the birds would dare. So the little snake, the Black Racer, said he would go through the water and bring back some fire. He swam across to the island and crawled through the grass to the tree and went in a small hole at the bottom. The heat and smoke were too much for him, too. After dodging about blindly over the hot ashes until he was almost on fire, he managed by good luck to get out again at the same hole. But his body had been scorched black. And he has ever since had the habit of darting and doubling back on his track, as if trying to escape from close quarters. He came back, and the great blacksnake, the Climber, offered to go for the fire. He swam over to the island and climbed up the tree on the outside as the blacksnake always does. But when he put his head down into the tree, the smoke choked him and he fell into the burning stump. Before he could climb out, he was as black as the little Black Racer.

Now the animals held another council, for still there was no fire and the world was cold. But birds, snakes and four-footed animals all had some excuse for not going. They were all afraid to venture near the burning sycamore tree. But the Water Spider at last said she would go. She was not the water spider that looks like a mosquito but the other one with black downy hair and red stripes on her body. She can run on top of the water or dive to the bottom. She would have no trouble getting to the island. But how could she bring back the fire?

"I'll manage that," said the Water Spider. Whereupon she spun a thread from her body and wove it into a bowl which she fastened to her back. Then she crossed to the island and went through the grass to where the fire was still burning. She put one little coal of fire into her bowl and came back with it. Ever since we have had fire, and the Water Spider still keeps her bowl.

How the Groundhog
Lost His Tail

Seven wolves once caught a Groundhog and said,
"Now we'll kill you and have something good to eat."
But the Groundhog said, "When you find good food,
you must rejoice over it, as people do in the Green
Corn Dance. I know you intend to kill me and I cannot
help myself. But if you want to dance, I'll sing for
you. I will show you a new dance. I'll lean against
seven trees in turn. At each you will dance away from
me and then, when I give a signal, turn and come back.
And at the last turn, you may kill me and eat me."

The wolves were very hungry. But they wanted to
learn the new dance, so they told the Groundhog to
go ahead. The Groundhog leaned against a tree and

began the song, "*Hawiyeehi.*" All the wolves danced away from him, until he gave the signal, "*Yu!*" and sang "*Hiyaguwe.*" Then they turned and danced back to him. "That's fine," said the Groundhog. And he went to the next tree and started the second song. The wolves danced away and then turned when he gave the signal and danced back again. "That's fine," said the Groundhog. And he went to another tree and began the third song.

The wolves danced their best, and the Groundhog encouraged them. But at the beginning of each new song, he moved to another tree that was a little nearer his hole under a stump.

At the seventh song, the Groundhog said, "Now, this is the last dance. When I say, '*Yu!*' you will all turn and come after me. The one who gets me may have me." With that, he began the seventh song. And he kept singing until the wolves had danced far away from him. Then he gave the signal, "*Yu!*" and made a jump for his hole. The wolves turned and chased after him. But he reached the hole first and dived in. Just as he got inside, the first wolf caught him by the tail and gave such a pull that it broke off. And the Groundhog's tail has been short ever since.

The Rabbit and the Possum
Seek a Wife

The Rabbit and the Possum each wanted a wife, but no one would marry either of them. They talked over the problem, and the Rabbit said, "We cannot get wives here. Let's go to the next town. I am the messenger for the council, and I will tell the people that I bring an order that everyone must marry at once. Then we'll be sure to get our wives."

The Possum thought this was a fine plan. So they started off together to the next town. Because the Rabbit traveled faster, he got there first. He waited outside until the people noticed him and took him into the townhouse. When the chief asked his business, the

Rabbit said he brought an order from the council that everybody must marry without delay. The chief called the people together and gave them the message. Every animal took a mate at once. And the Rabbit got a wife.

The Possum traveled so slowly that he got to the town after all the animals were married, leaving no wife for him. The Rabbit pretended to feel sorry for him and said, "Never mind. I'll carry the message to the people in the *next* town. You hurry on as fast as you can. This time you will get a wife."

So the Rabbit went to the next town, and the Possum followed close behind him. But when the Rabbit got to the townhouse, he told the people that, because there had been peace so long that everybody was getting lazy, the council had ordered that there must be a war at once. And he said it must begin right there in the townhouse. So the animals all began fighting, as they were told. But the Rabbit made four great leaps and got away, just as the Possum came in.

Everybody jumped on the Possum. He had not thought to bring weapons on a wedding trip, so he could not defend himself. After the animals had nearly beaten the life out of him, he fell over and pretended to be dead, until he saw a good chance to jump up and get away.

The Possum never got a wife. But he remembered the lesson, and ever since he shuts his eyes and pretends to be dead whenever a hunter has him in a close corner.

How the Terrapin
Beat the Rabbit

The Rabbit was a great runner, and everybody knew it. No one thought the Terrapin was anything but a slow traveler. But he was a great warrior and very boastful, and he and the Rabbit were always disputing about their speed. At last, they agreed to decide who was the faster by running a race. They chose the day and a starting place and agreed to run across four mountain ridges to a finish line.

The Rabbit felt so sure of winning that he said to the Terrapin, "You know you can't run. You can never win the race. So I will give you a head start.

You may start at the top of the first ridge. Then you'll have only three to cross, while I go over four."

The Terrapin said that that would be all right. But that night, when he went home to his family, he sent for his terrapin friends and told them he wanted their help. He said he knew he could not outrun the Rabbit, but he wanted to stop the Rabbit's boasting. He ex-

plained his plan to his friends. And they agreed to help him.

When the day of the race came, all the animals went out to watch. The Rabbit was with them. But the Terrapin had gone ahead toward the top of the first ridge, as he and the Rabbit had agreed. The animals could hardly see him, away in the tall grass.

The starting signal was given. The Rabbit ran with long jumps up the mountain, expecting to win the race before the Terrapin could get down the far side of that first ridge. But before the Rabbit got to the top of the mountain, he saw the Terrapin go over the ridge ahead of him. He ran on. When he reached the top, he looked around, but he could not see the Terrapin.

The Rabbit ran down the far side of the mountain and began to climb the second ridge. But when he looked up, there was the Terrapin just going over the top! The Rabbit was greatly surprised and made his longest jumps to catch up. But when he got to the top of that second ridge, there was the Terrapin, again far out in front, going over the third ridge! The Rabbit was getting tired now. He was nearly out of breath. But he kept on down the mountain and up the third

40

ridge. He got to the top, just in time to see the Terrapin cross the fourth ridge and win the race!

The Rabbit could not make another jump. He fell over on the ground, crying, "Mi! mi! mi! mi!" as the Rabbit has done ever since when he is too tired to run any more.

The Terrapin was named the winner of the race— although all the animals wondered how he had won against the Rabbit.

The Terrapin kept quiet and never told. But it had been easy enough to win. All the Terrapin's friends looked just alike. He had placed one of them near the top of each ridge to wait until the Rabbit came in sight and then to climb over the ridge and hide in the long grass on the far side. As the Rabbit reached the top of each ridge, he would see a Terrapin going over the next ridge ahead. And though he could hardly believe his eyes, he thought his rival was always one ridge ahead of him. But, of course, it was not his rival he saw each time. It was one of his rival's friends.

Where was the Terrapin? Why, all the while, he was near the top of the fourth ridge, where he had gone before the race began. When the Rabbit ran over the third ridge, the Terrapin had simply popped over the fourth ridge and waddled down to the finish line, so that he would appear to be the one who won the race—and could answer questions if the animals suspected anything!

How the Turkey Got His Beard

When the Terrapin won the race from the Rabbit, all the animals talked about it. They had always thought the Terrapin was slow, although they knew he was a great warrior and had many magic secrets besides. But the Turkey was not satisfied. He told the others that there must have been some trick to it. Said he, "I know the Terrapin can't run—he can hardly crawl—and I am going to prove it."

So, one day, the Turkey met the Terrapin coming home from war with a fresh scalp hanging from his neck and dragging on the ground. The Turkey laughed at the sight and said, "That scalp doesn't look right on

you. Your neck is too short and low down to wear it that way. Let me show you how to wear it."

The Terrapin agreed and gave the scalp to the Turkey, who fastened it around his neck.

"Now," said the Turkey, "I'll walk a little way, and you can see how it looks."

So the Turkey walked ahead a short distance and then turned and asked the Terrapin how he thought the scalp looked.

"It looks very nice," said the Terrapin. "It becomes you."

"Now I'll fix it a different way and let you see how it looks," said the Turkey. So he gave the string another pull and walked ahead again.

"Oh, that looks very nice," said the Terrapin.

But the Turkey kept on walking. When the Terrapin called to him to bring back the scalp, he only walked faster and soon broke into a run. Then the Terrapin got out his bow and by his magic art shot a number of cane splints into the Turkey's legs to cripple him, so that he could not run. This is why there are so many small bones in the Turkey's legs that are of no use whatever. But the Terrapin never caught the Turkey, who still wears the scalp hanging from his neck.

The Rabbit and
the Tar Wolf

Once there was such a long spell of dry weather that there was no more water in the creeks and springs. The animals held a council to see what to do about it. They decided to dig a well and all agreed to help, except the Rabbit, who was a lazy fellow and said, "I don't need to dig for water. The dew on the grass is enough for me."

The others did not like this, but they went to work together and dug their well. They noticed that the Rabbit kept sleek and lively, although it was still dry weather and the water was getting low in the well. They said, "That tricky Rabbit steals our water at night."

So they made a wolf of pine gum and tar and set it up by the well to scare the thief. That night the Rabbit came, as he had been coming every night, to drink enough to last him all the next day. He saw the queer black thing by the well and said, "Who's there?"

The tar wolf said nothing. The Rabbit came nearer, but the wolf never moved. So the Rabbit grew braver and said, "Get out of my way, or I'll strike you." Still the wolf never moved—and the Rabbit came up and struck it with his paw. The gum held his foot and it stuck fast.

Now the Rabbit was angry and said, "Let me go, or I'll kick you." Still the wolf said nothing. Then the Rabbit struck again with his hind foot so hard that it was caught in the gum and he could not move. And there he stuck until the animals came for water in the morning. When they found who the thief was they had great sport over him for a while and then got ready to kill him. One proposed cutting his head off. This the Rabbit said would be useless, because it had often been tried without hurting him. Other methods were proposed for killing him, all of which he said would be useless. At last, it was proposed to let him loose to perish in a thicket. Upon this the Rabbit pretended great uneasiness, and he pled hard for his life. His enemies, however, refused to listen, and he was let loose in the thicket. As soon as he was out of reach, he gave a whoop and bounding away, he exclaimed, "This is where I live!"

Why the Mole
Lives Underground

A man was in love with a woman who disliked him
and would have nothing to do with him. He tried
every way to win her favor, but he could not please
her. At last he grew so discouraged that he made himself sick thinking about it. The Mole came along and
asked what was the trouble. The man told him the
whole story. When the man had finished, the Mole
said, "I can help you, so that she not only will like
you but will come to you of her own will."

So that night, the Mole burrowed his way under-
ground to where the girl was in bed asleep and took
out her heart. He came back by the same way and

gave the heart to the man, but the man could not see
it even when it was put in his hand.

"There," said the Mole, "swallow it, and she will
come to you. She will not be able to stay away."

The man swallowed the heart. When the girl awoke,
she somehow thought at once of him and felt a strange
desire to be near him. She felt she must go to him at
once. She wondered and could not understand it, because she had always disliked him before. But, at last,
the feeling grew so strong that she was compelled to

go to the man and tell him she loved him and wanted to be his wife. Soon they were married. But all the medicine men who had known them both were surprised and wondered how it had come about. When they found that the girl's love for the man was the work of the Mole, whom they always before had thought too insignificant for their notice, they were very jealous and threatened to kill him. So he hid himself under the ground and never since has dared to come up to the surface.

How the Deer Got His Horns

In the beginning, the Deer had no horns. His head was smooth, just like the doe's. He was a great runner. The Rabbit was a great jumper. And the animals were all curious to know which could go farther in the same time. The animals talked about it a good deal. At last, they arranged a contest between the Deer and the Rabbit and made a nice pair of antlers as a prize for the winner. The Deer and the Rabbit were to start together from one side of a thicket, go through it, then turn and come back. The one who came out first was to get the horns.

On the day chosen for the match, all the animals

were there. The antlers were laid on the ground at the edge of the thicket to mark the starting point. While everybody was admiring the horns, the Rabbit said, "I don't know this part of the country. I want to take a look through the bushes where I am going to run."

The animals thought that was all right. So the Rabbit went into the thicket. But he was gone so long that, at last, the animals suspected he must be up to one of his tricks. They sent a messenger to look for him. The messenger found him, away in the middle of the thicket, gnawing down the bushes and pulling them away until he had a road cleared nearly to the other side.

The messenger turned around quietly and came back and told the other animals. When the Rabbit came out of the thicket, they accused him of cheating. He denied it, until they went into the thicket and found the cleared road. They agreed that such a trickster had no right to enter the race at all. So they gave the horns to the Deer, who was named the best runner, and he has worn them ever since. They told the Rabbit that, as he was so fond of cutting down bushes, he might thereafter do that for a living—and so he does to this day.

Why the Deer's Teeth
Are Blunt

The Rabbit was angry because the Deer had won the horns on the day the two were to race. So the Rabbit planned to get even.

One day, soon after the race, the Rabbit stretched a large grapevine across the trail and gnawed it nearly in two in the middle. Then he went back a little way, took a good run, and jumped up at the vine. He kept on running and jumping up at the vine, until the Deer came along and asked him what he was doing.

"Don't you see?" said the Rabbit. "I'm so strong I can bite through that grapevine at one jump."

The Deer could hardly believe this and wanted to see it done. So the Rabbit ran back, made a tremendous spring and bit through the vine where he had gnawed it before. The Deer, when he saw that, said, "Well, if you can do it, I can."

So the Rabbit stretched another thick grapevine across the trail—but without gnawing it in the middle. The Deer ran back, as he had seen the Rabbit do, made a spring and struck the grapevine right in the middle. But the vine only flew back and threw him over on his head. He tried again and again until he was all bruised and bleeding.

"Let me see your teeth," at last said the Rabbit. So the Deer showed the Rabbit his teeth, which were long like a wolf's teeth but not very sharp.

"No wonder you can't do it," said the Rabbit. "Your teeth are too blunt to bite anything. Let me sharpen them for you like mine. My teeth are so sharp that I can cut through a stick just like a knife." And he showed the Deer a black locust twig that, in rabbit fashion, he had shaved off as well as a knife could do. The Deer thought the Rabbit's idea was good. So the Rabbit got a hard stone with rough edges and filed and filed at the Deer's teeth, until they were worn down almost to the gums.

"It hurts," said the Deer. But the Rabbit said it

always hurt a little when the teeth began to get sharp. So the Deer kept quiet.

After much filing, the Rabbit said, "Now try to bite the vine." So the Deer tried again. But this time he could not bite at all.

"Now you've paid for your horns," said the Rabbit, as he jumped away through the bushes. Ever since then, the Deer's teeth have been so blunt that he cannot chew anything but grass and leaves.

How the Redbird
Got His Color

A Raccoon passing a Wolf one day made several insulting remarks. At last the Wolf grew angry and turned and chased the Raccoon. The Raccoon ran his fastest and reached a tree by the riverside before the Wolf could catch him. He climbed the tree and stretched out on a limb overhanging the river.

When the Wolf arrived, he saw the Raccoon's reflection in the water. Thinking it was the Raccoon, the Wolf jumped at it—and was nearly drowned before he could scramble out of the river, all wet and dripping. He lay down on the bank to dry and fell asleep. While the Wolf was sleeping, the Raccoon

came down the tree and plastered his eyes with mud. When the Wolf awoke, he found he could not open his eyes, and he began to whine.

Just then, a little brown bird came through the bushes. The bird heard the Wolf crying and asked what was the matter. The Wolf told the bird what had happened and said, "If you will get my eyes open, I will show you where to find some nice red paint to paint yourself."

"All right," said the brown bird. So he pecked at the Wolf's eyes until he got off all the plaster. Then the Wolf took him to a rock that had streaks of bright red paint running through it. The little bird painted himself with it and has ever since been a Redbird.

Why the Terrapin's Shell Is Scarred

The Possum and the Terrapin went out together to hunt persimmons and found a tree full of ripe fruit. The Possum climbed the tree and began throwing the persimmons down to the Terrapin. A wolf came along and began to snap at the persimmons as they fell before the Terrapin could reach them. The Possum awaited his chance and then threw down a large persimmon that lodged in the wolf's throat and choked him to death.

"I'll take his ears for hominy spoons," said the Terrapin.

The Terrapin cut off the wolf's ears and started

home with them, leaving the Possum still eating persimmons up in the tree.

After a while, the Terrapin came to a house and was invited to have some corn broth. He sat out before the house in the sunshine and dipped up the broth with one of the wolf's ears for a spoon. The people noticed and wondered. When he had eaten all the broth he wanted, he went on. Soon he came to another house and was asked to have some more broth. He dipped it up again with the wolf's ear, until he had had enough. Soon the news went around that the Terrapin had killed the wolf and was using his ears for spoons.

All the wolves got together and followed the Terrapin's trail until they caught up with him and made him prisoner. Then they held a council to decide what to do with him. They all agreed to boil him in a clay pot. They brought a pot, but the Terrapin only laughed at it and said that, if they put him into that thing, he would kick it all to pieces. So they said that, instead, they would burn him in the fire. But the Terrapin laughed again and said he would put the fire out. Then they said they would throw him into the deepest hole in the river and drown him. The Terrapin begged and begged them not to do that. But they paid no attention to him and dragged him to the river and threw him in. That was just what the Terrapin had been waiting for all the time. He dived under the water and came up on the other side and got away.

But some say that when he was thrown into the river, he struck a rock which broke his back in a dozen places. They say he sang a medicine song:

"I have sewed myself together.

I have sewed myself together."

And the pieces came together, but the scars remain on his shell to this day.

How the Rabbit Stole
the Otter's Coat

The animals were of different sizes and wore coats of various colors and patterns. Some wore long fur and others wore short. Some had rings on their tails and some had no tails at all. Some had coats of brown, others of black or yellow. They were always arguing about their good looks. So, at last, they agreed to hold a council to decide who had the finest coat.

They had heard a great deal about the Otter, who lived so far up the creek that he seldom came down to visit the other animals. It was said that he had the finest coat of all. But no one knew just what it was like, because it had been a long time since anyone had seen him. The other animals did not even know exactly where he lived, only the general direction. But they knew he would come to the council when the word got out.

Now, the Rabbit wanted to be chosen the best dressed. So when it began to look as though the Otter might be judged to have the finest coat, the Rabbit made a plan to cheat the Otter out of the prize. He asked a few sly questions until he learned what trail the Otter would take to the council place. Then, without saying anything to anyone, he went on ahead and after four day's travel, he met the Otter. He knew the Otter at once by the Otter's beautiful coat of soft, dark brown fur.

The Otter was glad to see the Rabbit and asked him where he was going.

"Oh," said the Rabbit, "the animals sent me to bring you to the council. Because you live so far away, they were afraid you might not know the road."

The Otter thanked the Rabbit, and they went on together. They traveled all day toward the council ground. At night, the Rabbit selected a camping place, because the Otter was a stranger in that part of the country. He cut down bushes for beds and fixed everything for comfort.

The next morning, they started again. In the afternoon, as they went along, the Rabbit began to pick up wood and bark and load it on his back. When the Otter asked what this was for, the Rabbit said it was to make them warm and comfortable at night. After a while, at sunset, they stopped and made their camp.

When supper was over, the Rabbit got a stick and shaved it down to a paddle. The Otter asked what that was for.

"I have good dreams when I sleep with a paddle under my head," said the Rabbit.

When the paddle was finished, the Rabbit began to cut away the bushes to make a clean trail down to the river. The Otter wondered more and more about the Rabbit's behavior and asked why he was making a path.

"This place is called The Place Where it Rains Fire," said the Rabbit. "Sometimes it rains fire here, and the sky looks a little that way tonight. You go to sleep, and I'll sit up and watch. If the fire does come, as soon as you hear me shout, you run and jump into

the river. Better hang your coat on a limb over there, so it won't get burned."

The Otter did as he was told, and they both doubled up to go to sleep. But the Rabbit kept awake. After a while, the fire died down to red coals. The Rabbit called, but the Otter was fast asleep and made no answer. In a little while, the Rabbit called again. But the Otter never stirred. Then the Rabbit filled the paddle with hot coals and threw them up into the air and shouted, "It's raining fire! It's raining fire!"

The hot coals fell all around the Otter, and he jumped up.

"To the water!" cried the Rabbit. And the Otter

ran and jumped into the river. And he has lived in the water ever since.

The Rabbit took the Otter's coat and put it on, leaving his own behind, and went on to the council. All the animals were there, and everyone was looking for the Otter. At last, they saw him in the distance. They said to each other, "The Otter is coming!" And they sent one of the small animals to show him to the best seat. They were all glad to see him and went up in turn to welcome him. But the Otter kept his head down with one paw over his face. The animals all wondered why he was so bashful, until the Bear came up and pulled the paw away. There, instead of the Otter, was the Rabbit with his split nose! He sprang up and started to run. The Bear struck at him and pulled his tail off, but the Rabbit was too quick for them all and got away. However, he left his tail behind him and has had only a stumpy one ever since.

Why the Possum's Tail Is Bare

The Possum used to have a long, bushy tail. He was so proud of it that he combed it out every morning and sang about it at every dance. The Rabbit, who had had no tail since the Bear pulled it out, became very jealous and made up his mind to play a trick on the Possum.

There was to be a great council and a dance at which all the animals were to be present. It was the Rabbit's business to send out the news. So as he was passing the Possum's place, he stopped to ask the Possum if he would be at the dance. The Possum said he would come if he could have a special seat.

"I have such a handsome tail," the Possum said, "that I ought to sit where everybody can see me."

The Rabbit promised him a special seat and promised also to send someone to comb and dress his tail for the dance. The Possum was very pleased.

Then the Rabbit went to the Cricket, who was such an expert hair cutter that people called him the barber. The Rabbit told him to go next morning and dress the Possum's tail for the dance that night. The Rabbit told the Cricket just what to do, and then went on about some other mischief.

In the morning, the Cricket went to the Possum's house and said he had come to get the Possum ready for the dance. So the Possum stretched himself out and shut his eyes, while the Cricket combed out his tail and wrapped a red string around it to keep it smooth until night. But all the time, as he wound the string around the Possum's tail, he was clipping off the hair close to the roots—and the Possum never knew it.

That night the Possum went to the townhouse, where the dance was to be held, and found the best seat ready for him, just as the Rabbit had promised. When his turn came to dance, he loosened the string from his tail and stepped to the middle of the floor. The drummers began to drum. And the Possum began to sing, "See my beautiful tail."

Everybody shouted, and the Possum danced around the circle and sang again, "See what a fine color it has." Everybody shouted again. And he danced around another time, singing, "See how it sweeps the ground."

The animals shouted more loudly than ever, and the Possum was delighted. He danced around again and sang, "See how fine the fur is."

Then everybody laughed so long that the Possum

wondered why. He looked around the circle of animals, and they were all laughing at him. Then he looked down at his beautiful tail and saw that there was not a hair left upon it. It was as bare as the tail of a lizard. He was so astonished and ashamed that he could not say a word, but rolled over helpless on the ground and grinned—as the Possum does to this day when taken by surprise.

GEORGE F. SCHEER

Cherokee Animal Tales is George F. Scheer's second book for young readers. His first was *Yankee Doodle Boy: A Young Soldier's Adventures in the American Revolution Told by Himself,* which won the 1964 Thomas Alva Edison Foundation National Mass Media Award for Special Excellence in Portraying America's Past.

Mr. Scheer has also written (with H. F. Rankin) *Rebels and Redcoats,* a major history of the American Revolution told largely in the words of participants. He has been General Editor of the Meridian Documents of American History, and has contributed to *Saturday Review, American Heritage,* and other publications. In recognition of his contribution to military history in 1960 he was made a Fellow of the Company of Military Historians.

He and his family live in Chapel Hill, North Carolina.

ROBERT FRANKENBERG

Robert Frankenberg has illustrated more than 100 books, including many works of folklore and American history for young people.

He was born and grew up in Mt. Vernon, New York, and studied at the Art Students League. He is now Head of the Drawing Department of the School of Visual Arts in New York City.